For my family,
and for everyone whose heart
has more than one home
—J.Y.

For anyone whose family
is changing shape:
love is like water, it fills up
whatever shape you pour it into
—C.O.

Two Homes, One Heart

Text copyright © 2024 by Jessica Young
Illustrations copyright © 2024 by Chelsea O'Byrne
All rights reserved. Manufactured in Italy.
No part of this book may be used or reproduced in any manner
whatsoever without written permission except in the case of
brief quotations embodied in critical articles and reviews. For
information address HarperCollins Children's Books, a division
of HarperCollins Publishers,
195 Broadway, New York, NY 10007.
www.harpercollinschildrens.com

Library of Congress Control Number: 2023937151
ISBN 978-0-06-325397-1

The artist used watercolor, pastels,
colored pencils, and digital tools to create
the digital illustrations for this book.
Hand lettering by Chelsea O'Byrne
Design by Whitney Leader-Picone
23 24 25 26 27 RTLO 10 9 8 7 6 5 4 3 2 1

First Edition

JESSICA YOUNG

CHELSEA O'BYRNE

TWO HOMES, ONE HEART

HARPER

An Imprint of HarperCollinsPublishers

Two homes,

one heart.

Once together,

now apart.

Different
views,

same
sky.

With hello

comes goodbye.

Two parents,
one me.

Are we still a family?

Whole
world

turned
around.

Something
lost,

something found.

Two houses,

one team.

Space to
stretch,

room to
dream.

Time to spend,

love to share.

Some here.

Some there.

Two voices,

one song.

Big hopes

growing
strong.

Old memories,

new start.

Two homes,

one
heart.